Muffin Mouse on the Go

by Lawrence DiFiori

A GOLDEN BOOK • NEW YORK
Western Publishing Company, Inc., Racine, Wisconsin 53404

Muffin Mouse likes to walk, so she is putting on her red walking sneakers.

She is going to walk to Bobo Muskrat's party. He lives on the other side of the pond.

Muffin Mouse takes her time.
The air is sweet, the birds are
singing, and the bees are buzzing.

On her way, Muffin sees her friend Frankie Frog in his boat. He is sailing swiftly across the pond.

Sally Snake scoots by
on her speedy skateboard.
Muffin waves.

Chip Chipmunk goes wheeling past Muffin on his brand-new bicycle.

Tom Turtle drives by in his
sports car.

Here comes Rufus Rat and his steam engine.

Overhead, Merle Mouse flies
her airplane.